THE CROCODILE WHO SWALLOWED THE SUN

ISBN : 978-1-988779-37-9

Dépôt légal : bibliothèque et archives nationales du Québec, 2020
Dépôt légal : bibliothèque et archives Canada, 2020

Publisher   : Open Book Publishing
Author   : Bachar Karroum   bachar.karroum@gmail.com
Illustrator   : Luis Peres   www.icreateworlds.net
Poetry Editor   : Tamara Rittershaus   www.PictureBookTamara.com
Proofreader (rhymes) : Jana Broecker
Proofreader (text)   : Lawrence Isabelle

Based on the classic story "Badna Al Shams"
(We Want The Sun) by "Sanabel Group"

In collaboration with
"Nasma Productions, LLC"

www.nasmaproductions.com

This book belongs to:

_____

Once a swampland crocodile
was boasting of his power:
"I am the strongest of the beasts.
I make the creatures cower!

Alone, I rule the animals.
No other shares my reign.
I 'll roam the land to see myself
how creatures fear my name."

Far from the swamp, the croc observed
a rooster's morning song.
The barnyard creatures praised the sun.
They danced and sang along:

"The sun alone can warm the earth
or make the flowers grow.
She proudly gives us light and life.
She's queen of all we know."

The crocodile got jealous
as he watched the barnyard friends.
"The sun does not deserve their praise!
Today this party ends!"

"I 'll steal their warmth and light," said Croc.
"I 'll spoil their morning fun!
Before the creatures wake today ...

"... I'll swallow up the sun."

His evil plan had worked so well,
the crocodile could say:
"I hold the power of the sun!
I'm KING of night and day!"

That day, the rooster waited long
to sing his morning song.
"The sun forgot to rise today!
Whatever could be wrong?"

The birds replied, "A crocodile!
It swallowed up the day!
Please, Rooster, fight the crocodile —
or NIGHT is here to stay."

To the swamp!" The rooster stomped
while spouting angry cries:
"I'll scratch that thief right on the nose.
I'll poke it in the eyes!"

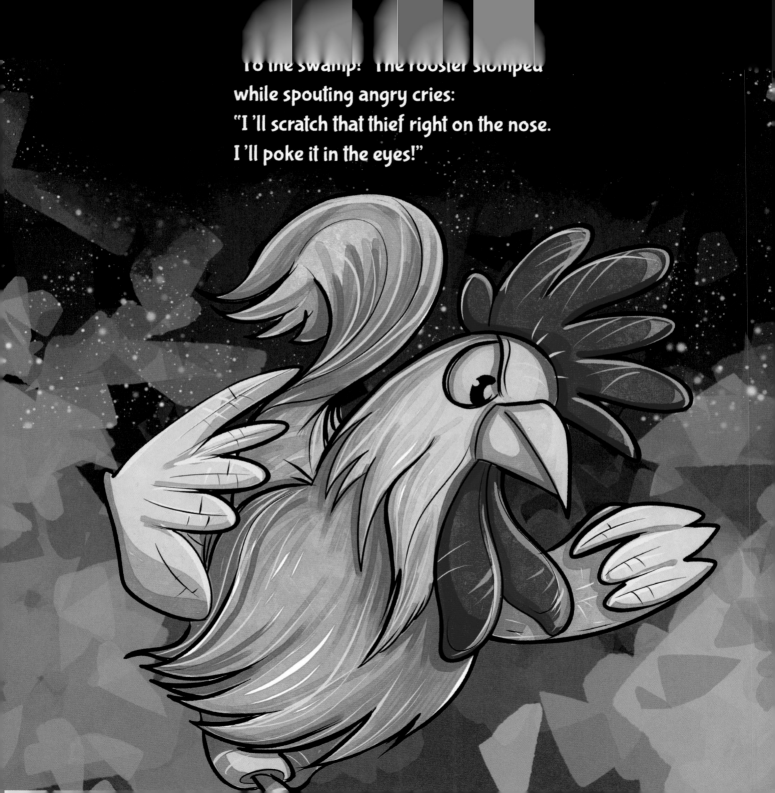

The croc slapped Rooster's legs so hard,
he limped off in defeat.
"Well, if you fought a crocodile,
you wanted to get beat!"

The rabbit cried, "It's much too dark.
It's hard to find my food.
Without my carrot snack today,
I'll have a nasty mood!"

When Rabbit tried to open up
the giant's toothy jaw,
the crocodile just swung his head
and knocked back Rabbit's paw.

As Rabbit hobbled off, she said,
"I 'll get us back our sun!"
With angry growl, the croc replied,
"Just save yourself and run!"

The goat was stumbling in the dark.
"This isn't any fun.
I'll fight that nasty crocodile!
I'll MAKE it share the sun!"

Goat scratched the dirt and braced his head.
"My horns will ram the beast."

The crocodile just moved aside.
He wasn't hurt the least.

Goat rammed a tree and rolled in mud.
"My horn! It broke in two!"
The croc just growled, "Get out of here,
or else I'll break you, too!"

"We'll never match its strength with force.
This thief's a mighty croc.
It's best we face the beast in peace
and have a little talk."

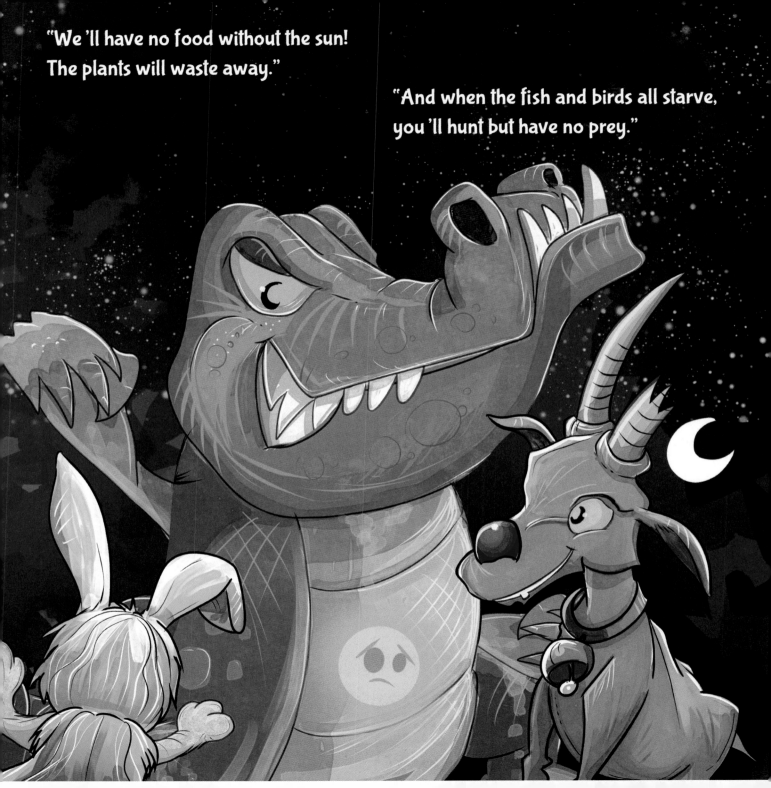

The stubborn crocodile just laughed.
He didn't want to hear.

"Their arguments are good," he thought,
"but kings don't live in fear.

The crocodiles have food to spare,
this begging is for show."
And though the sun was burning Croc,
he would not let it go.

The birds all left the swampland
as each day grew colder still.
The plants and fish were dying from
the water's icy chill.

The croc knew he'd been warned before
by every barnyard friend
"I must admit they're right," he thought.
"We might soon meet our end."

When Croc's young brother had no food,
he realized the harm he'd done.
At last, the croc agreed
to open up and free the sun.

He walked away to find some space.
The whole world heard his groan,
as Crocodile released the sun
to take its rightful throne.

"The barnyard was impacted
when I stole the sun away,
but even mighty crocodiles
still need the light of day."

Now Rabbit, Goat, and Donkey sing
with Rooster's crow each dawn:
"We celebrate the light of day,
for once, our sun was gone!"

We couldn't win with force alone,
nor take the sun by might.
We taught the greedy crocodile
that creatures share the light."

The crocodile now joins the friends
in singing to the sun
because he learned that sharing light
is best for everyone.

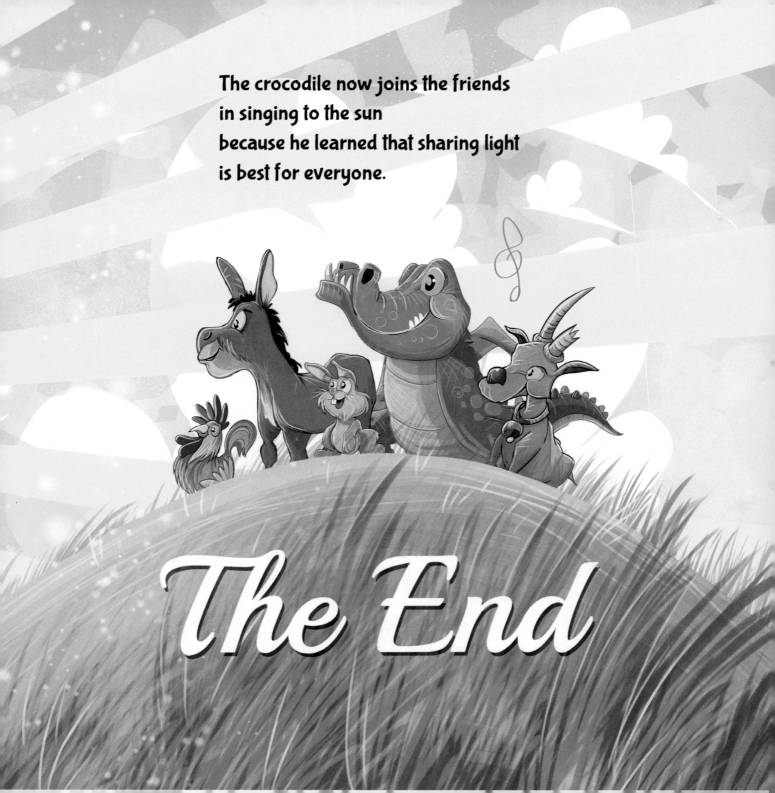

The End

Made in the USA
Columbia, SC
06 February 2021